For Steve, with love always
~ J.B.

For Sophie and Grace, with love
~ R.B.

Library of Congress Cataloging-in-Publication Data is available.

ISBN-13: 978-0-545-03408-1
ISBN-10: 0-545-03408-6

10 9 8 7 6 5 4 3 2 1   8 9 10 11 12/0

Printed in Singapore
First Scholastic US printing, January 2008

Mommy's Little Star

Written by
Janet Bingham

Illustrated by
Rosalind Beardshaw

Cartwheel
·B·O·O·K·S· ®

SCHOLASTIC INC.

New York   Toronto   London   Auckland   Sydney
Mexico City   New Delhi   Hong Kong   Buenos Aires

Little Fox was chasing the falling leaves.
Every time he caught one, another one fell.
"I'm going to catch them all!" he panted.

"It might be hard to catch every one," said Mommy Fox. "There are too many. Look at all the leaves waiting to fall."

Little Fox stared up at the leafy branches.
"There are trees full of leaves," he sang,
"right up high to the top of the sky!"

"Not quite to the top," said Mommy Fox, tickling Little Fox's nose. "The sky doesn't stop there. Something goes even higher than the trees."

"What goes higher?" asked Little Fox.

"Bees!" said Mommy Fox.
"Watch them!"
A family of bees
bumbled away, over
the top of the trees.

"Bzzzz," said Little Fox.
"I'm a bee, buzz, buzz,
buzzing at the top of
the sky!"

"So does the sky stop there?" Little Fox asked.
Mommy Fox whisked away a nosy bumblebee.
"No, not there," she said. "What flies higher than
the bees? Do you know?"

"Birds go higher!" shouted Little Fox.
"And I'm a bird, flying high to
the top of the sky!"

Little Fox fell and landed with a bump.
"Is that the top?" he asked.
"Does the sky
stop there?"

Mommy Fox kissed him better.
"No, not there," she said. "What
goes higher than the birds,
but only after rain?"

"The rainbow!" laughed Little Fox.
"Look at me now! I'm dancing on
the rainbow, up above all the birds
and trees and bees.
"Is that the top?" he asked.
"Does the sky stop there?"

Mommy Fox shook her head.
"Something goes over the rainbow,"
she said.

"What does?" asked Little Fox.
"Tell me, Mommy!"

"Clouds!" said Mommy Fox.
"The clouds float high and far.
And look, they are showing us
the way home."

Little Fox watched the clouds drifting by. "Let's follow them!" he cried. And he set off running and tumbling toward the den.

The sun was setting by the time they reached home.

"Good night, sun!" said Little Fox. "I know you go higher than the clouds, but you're not high now."

"That's true," said Mommy Fox. "The sun is going to bed, just like you. It will climb high in the sky again tomorrow. But look . . ."

". . . Here comes the moon
to shine in its place."
Little Fox watched the
moon brighten overhead.
"I can almost touch it," he said,
"even though it's so high."

"That must be the top," Little Fox said. "Does the sky stop there?"

"No, not there," said Mommy Fox. "What do you think shines even higher than the moon?"

Little Fox looked at the twinkling sky.
"Stars!" he laughed. "The stars shine higher."
He started to count them as they turned on their
lights. "There are so many stars!" he sighed.

"So many beautiful stars," agreed Mommy Fox. Little Fox yawned. "So that's the top," he said. "The sky stops there."

"Not even there," said Mommy Fox. "You see, there is no top. . . ."

". . . The stars shine down from the deep,
dark, quiet sky that goes on and on forever."
Little Fox gazed up into the darkness.
He felt warm and safe with Mommy Fox beside him.
"So the sky goes on and on forever,"
he whispered sleepily. "But where does it start?"

Mommy Fox hugged him closer.
"The sky is just like love," she said.
"It never ends.

And it starts right here . . ."

". . . with my own little star."